Written by
JULIA
DONALDSON

Illustrated by
SARA
OGILVIE

The HOSPITAL DOG

MACMILLAN CHILDREN'S BOOKS

Here is a dog, a Dalmatian called Dot.
Is she quite ordinary? NO, SHE'S NOT!

Here is Dot's owner, a lady called Rose,
With rings on her fingers and specs on her nose.

After their breakfast of porridge and tea,
Rose and her dog always swim in the sea.

Then they hop onto bus number seventy eight,

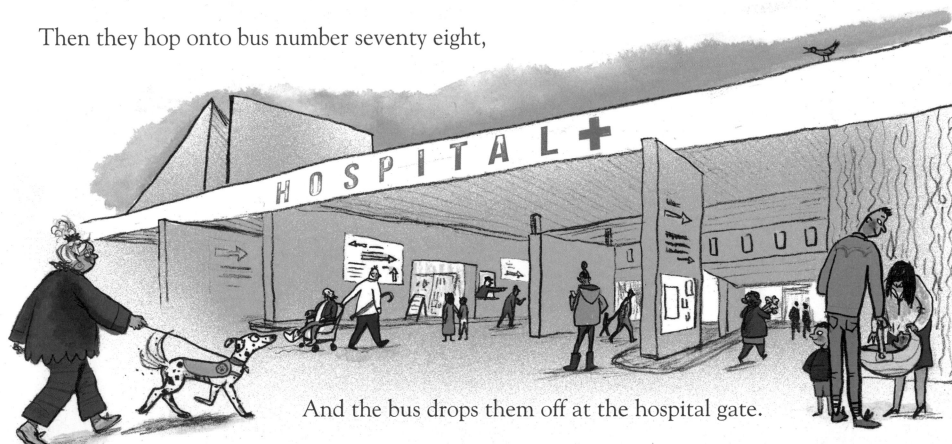

And the bus drops them off at the hospital gate.

Here are the children in Wallaby Ward,
Most of them happy but some of them bored.

A girl's feeling shy and a baby is howling,
A toddler's cross and a teenager's scowling.
A visitor's jumping about like a frog.
But look who's arrived . . .

It's the hospital dog!

Bea's feeling nervous. Today's her first day.
She wonders how long she'll be going to stay.

There's a tear in her eye and an ache in her head . . .

But look who's appeared on the chair by her bed!

A pat and a stroke and a cuddle with Dot.
Is Bea feeling scared still? NO, SHE'S NOT!

Gus, who is older than all of the others,
Would rather be out playing ball with his brothers.

He's read all his books and he's tired of TV . . .

But here is a dog he's delighted to see!

A pat and a stroke and a cuddle with Dot.
Is Gus feeling bored still? NO, HE'S NOT!

Here's baby Katy. She's hot, and what's more
She's covered in spots and her tummy is sore.
It seems that she'll never stop crying – boo hoo!

Till Dot lifts a paw to say, "How do you do?"

A pat and a stroke and a cuddle with Dot.

Is Katy still crying? NO, SHE'S NOT!

Dot gets a hat and makes friends with a bear.

She plays with a ball and she rides in a chair.

She calms down a doctor;

she cheers up a mummy.

She lets little Tyler play Tickle Dot's Tummy.

Here is a boy who is deaf. He's called Joe.
Rose helps her dog make the sign for "hello".

Joe's going home now. His cough is much better.
His mum packs his toothbrush and Dot packs his sweater.

Dot's going home too. The ward round is done.
She's sorry to leave – but the lift ride is fun.

Off to the bus stop go five pairs of feet.

Then Joe sees a friend and steps into the street!

Here comes a car, but he can't hear it come.

Rose isn't watching, and nor is Joe's mum.

Dot rushes out and she pushes Joe back,

But the car hits her leg with a sudden loud

SMACK!

A trip to the vet, and an X-ray for Dot.
Is Dot feeling happy? NO, SHE'S NOT!

The vet says, "Don't worry. It's not a disaster.
The leg will be fine after six weeks in plaster."

Six weeks to wait! That's a very long time.
Dot has a limp, and she can't jump or climb.

No swimming!

No bus rides!

Dot's feeling bored.

But here come the children from Wallaby Ward!
Joe, Bea and Katy, Tyler and Gus.
"We're visiting you, like you visited us!"

A pat and a stroke and a biscuit for Dot.
Is she enjoying it? YES – A LOT!

For Hospital Dog Nala, and her owner Sandy ~ JD

For the carers and canines who help make us feel better ~ SO

First published 2020 by Macmillan Children's Books
an imprint of Pan Macmillan
The Smithson, 6 Briset Street, London EC1M 5NR
Associated companies throughout the world.
www.panmacmillan.com

ISBN: 978-1-5098-6831-5

1 3 5 7 9 8 6 4 2

A CIP catalogue record for this book
is available from the British Library.

Printed in Italy